SKY WATC

When it comes to being bored, the sky's the limit for Nancy!

Dyan Sheldon is a children's writer, adult novelist, humorist and cat-lover. Her children's titles include *A Witch Got on at Paddington Station*, *The Whales' Song* and, for Walker Books, *A Night to Remember*, *Harry and Chicken*, *Harry the Explorer* and *Harry's Holiday*, as well as the picture books *I Forgot* and *Love, Your Bear Pete*.

Graham Percy's many picture books include Alison Uttley's Sam Pig stories and, for Walker, *When Dad Cuts Down the Chestnut Tree*, *When Dad Fills in the Garden Pond*, *Reynard the Fox*, *A Cup of Starshine* and *The Cock, the Mouse and the Little Red Hen*.

Some other titles

The Baked Bean Kids
by Ann Pilling / Derek Matthews

The Finger-eater
by Dick King-Smith / Arthur Robins

The Haunting of Pip Parker
by Anne Fine / Emma Chichester Clark

Holly and the Skyboard
by Ian Whybrow/ Tony Kenyon

Jolly Roger
by Colin McNaughton

A Night to Remember
by Dyan Sheldon / Robert Crowther

Tillie McGillie's Fantastical Chair
by Vivian French / Sue Heap

The Unknown Planet
by Jean Ure / Chris Winn

DYAN SHELDON

SKY WATCHING

Illustrations by
Graham Percy

WALKER BOOKS
LONDON

First published 1992 by
Walker Books Ltd, 87 Vauxhall Walk
London SE11 5HJ

This edition published 1994

2 4 6 8 10 9 7 5 3 1

Printed in England

British Library Cataloguing in Publication Data
A catalogue record for this book is available from the British Library.

ISBN 0-7445-3104-7

CONTENTS

Chapter One
9

Chapter Two
21

Chapter Three
31

Chapter Four
41

Chapter Five
53

CHAPTER ONE

Once upon a time, there was a little girl called Nancy.

Nancy wasn't a bad little girl, but she was easily bored.

No matter what Nancy played with, or what she did, she soon grew tired of it. Then she crossed her arms and stamped her foot. She scowled and threw things round the room.

"This is no fun any more!" cried Nancy. "I've got nothing to do! I'm bored, bored, bored!"

To stop Nancy from being bored, her parents bought her things.

"We'll buy you so many toys that you'll never be bored again," they promised.

They bought her everything they could think of: games and bicycles; balls and building blocks and model trains; story books and colouring pens and tiny planes that really flew; bags of stuffed animals and boxes full of smiling dolls.

Nancy crossed her arms and stamped her foot. She scowled. "I'm still bored," said Nancy.

Soon, Nancy had so many things that she had no more room for them.

If you squeezed through the door of Nancy's bedroom there was nowhere to walk. If you pushed your way to the bed there was nowhere to sit. If you opened the

cupboard, toys fell on your head.

"I'm still bored," said Nancy. Her parents bought her more toys.

Soon Nancy had so many things that there was no more room in the house at all.

The sofa disappeared under a mountain of games. The kitchen table vanished beneath a sea of books. There were so many toys in

the hall that Nancy's gran, who had come for a visit, got lost walking through the front door.

Nancy stamped her foot. There were plenty of things to throw, but nowhere to throw them. "I'm still bored," scowled Nancy. "I'm very, very bored."

CHAPTER TWO

Nancy's parents didn't know what to do.

"What shall we do?" asked Nancy's father.

"What *can* we do?" asked Nancy's mother.

"I'll tell you what I'd do," said a small, faraway voice.

Nancy's parents looked at one another.

"Who said that?" asked Nancy's parents.

"I said that!" snapped the small, faraway voice. A bony hand appeared from under a pile of dolls and teddy bears. It was Nancy's gran.

Everyone had forgotten about her, she'd been lost for so long. Nancy's parents helped her out.

"What *would* you do?" Nancy asked her grandmother. "Send me to bed without any supper?"

"Then you'd be hungry as well as bored," said Nancy's gran.

Nancy crossed her arms. "Are you going to stop me from watching telly?"

"No one's seen the telly in weeks," said Nancy's gran. "There wouldn't be much point in that."

Nancy stamped her foot. "I know!" cried Nancy. "You're going to take away all my toys!"

"What for?" asked her grandmother. "You don't play with them anyway."

Nancy frowned. "Well, if you're not doing any of those things, what are you going to do?"

Nancy's gran climbed down from the hillock of bicycles she'd been sitting on. "I'm going to make you sit in the sky until you've learned your lesson," she said.

Nancy wasn't too keen on sitting in the sky.

What could be more boring than that?

"There's nothing to do in the sky," she complained.

Nancy's gran brought out a ladder. "Nothing?" she asked.

"Nothing," said Nancy.

"Then just look," said Nancy's gran.

Nancy scowled. "But there's nothing to look at."

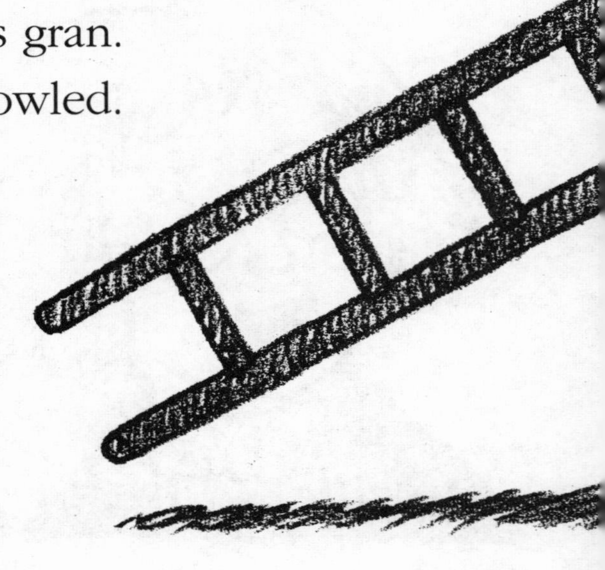

Gran gave her a shove up the ladder. “I’m sure you’ll find something,” said Nancy’s gran, pulling the ladder away.

Nancy sat down on a cloud and began to cry.

CHAPTER THREE

After a while Nancy grew tired of crying when there was no one to hear her and beg her to stop.

"This isn't any fun," she sniffed. "Crying is boring, too."

She leaned over a cloud and called to her grandmother. "Can I come down now?" she asked. "I'm sure I've learned my lesson."

Nancy's gran appeared on the lawn. She was riding Nancy's skateboard. "What do you see in the sky?" she asked.

"Clouds," answered Nancy. "Lots of clouds."

"And what do they look like?" asked her gran.

"They're white," said Nancy. "They're big and white."

Her grandmother frowned. "You're not ready yet," she said and she rolled back into the house.

Nancy watched the sky a little more closely after that. There was certainly nothing else to do.

A flock of birds hurried by. I wonder where they're going, thought Nancy.

Maybe they'll land under a palm tree on a tropical island.

Maybe they'll land in a colony of penguins at the South Pole.

Someone waved to Nancy from a passing plane.

Nancy waved back.

I wonder where they're going, thought Nancy. Maybe they were going to Europe, or Africa. Maybe they were going to the very top of the world.

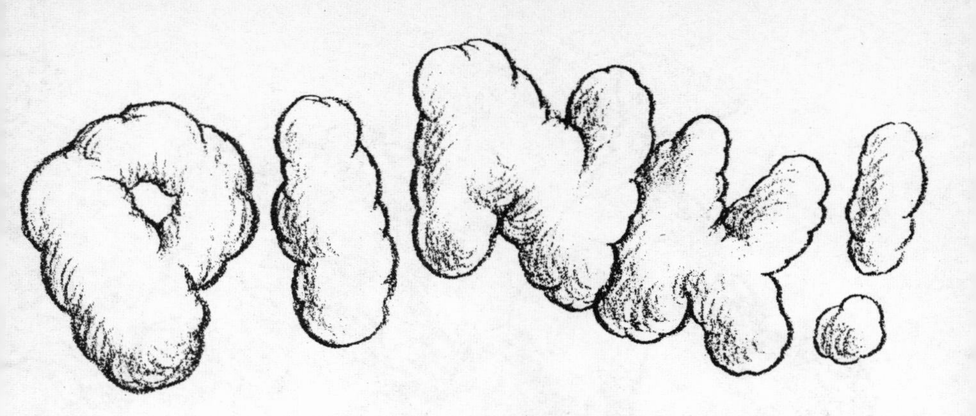

As she watched the sky, Nancy noticed that not all of the clouds were white. Some were pink, or purple, or even green.

"Wow!" said Nancy. "Green clouds. They're great."

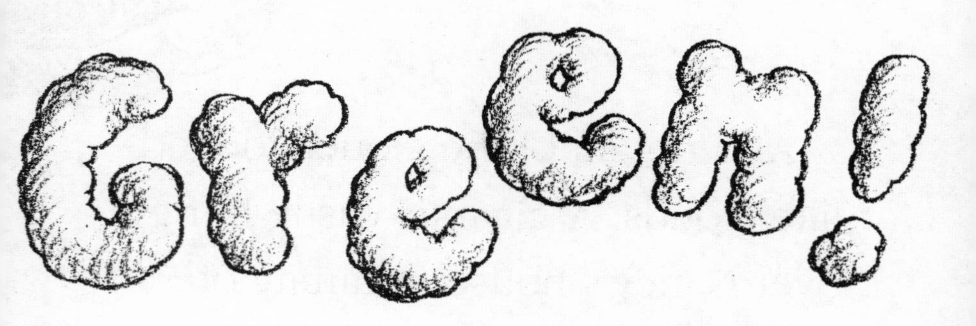

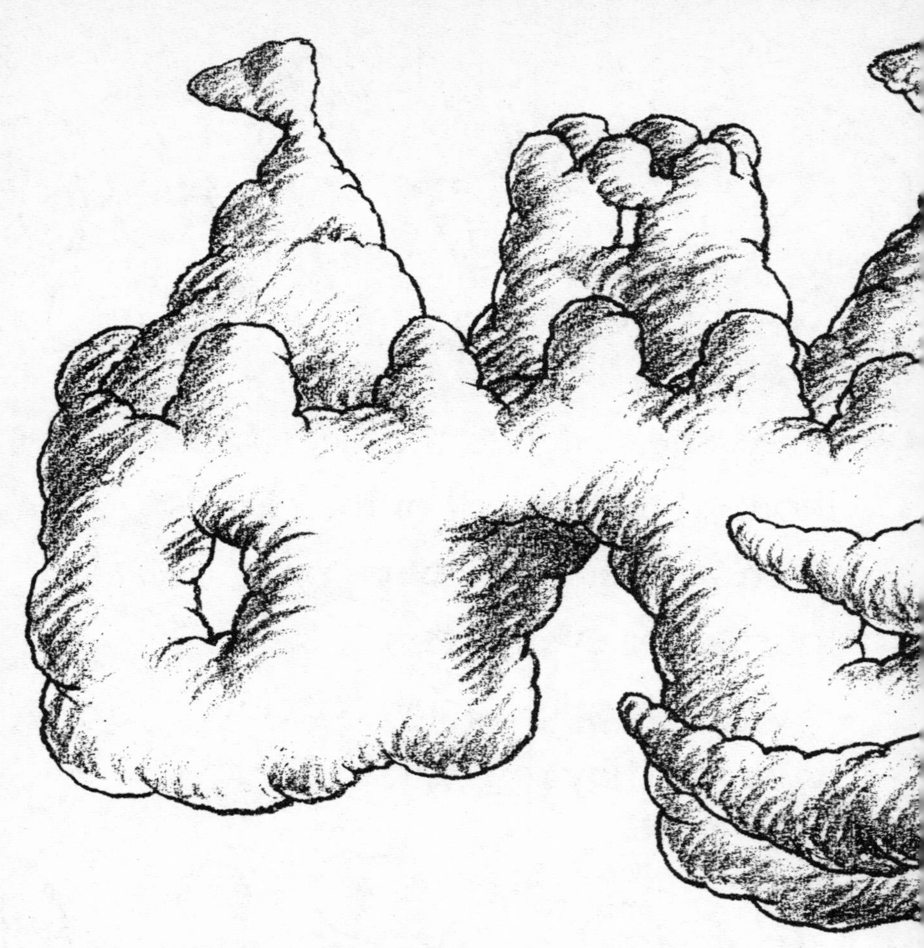

And not all of the clouds looked like clouds. A gigantic castle hung over Nancy's house. A family of dinosaurs floated past her head.

"Hey!" shouted Nancy, ducking out of the way. "There goes a brontosaurus!"

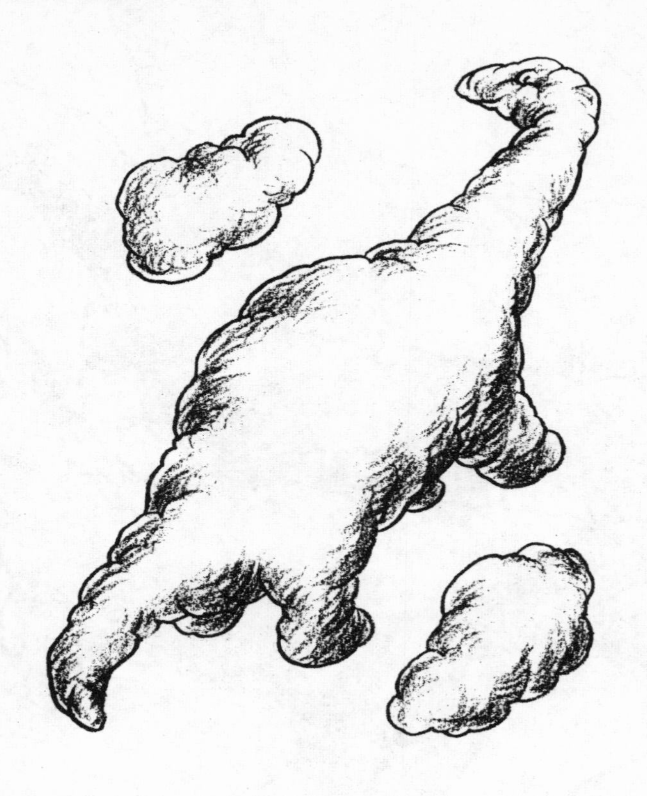

CHAPTER FOUR

Night fell. Nancy's gran came out into the garden on Nancy's pogo stick.

"Nancy!" she shouted. "Nancy! Are you still there?"

Nancy peered over a giant turkey. "Here I am!" called Nancy. "I've been sliding on the clouds."

"It's getting late," said Nancy's grandmother. "Have you learned your lesson yet?"

Nancy blinked in surprise. She'd been so busy that she hadn't realized how dark it was. Suddenly, she wanted to be in her nice warm house, having her tea.

"Oh, yes," said Nancy. "I'm sure I've learned my lesson. The sky isn't boring at all. It's filled with all sorts of interesting things. Can I come down?"

"Not so fast!" said Nancy's grandmother. "First tell me what you see now."

Nancy looked around. "I see the moon and stars," said Nancy.

"And what do they look like?" asked her gran.

Nancy shrugged.
"They don't look like anything," said Nancy. "Just the moon and stars."

Nancy's gran sighed. "You're not ready yet," she said and she hopped back into the house.

Nancy sat down. She stared into the night.

Twinkle, twinkle little star, thought Nancy, *what a boring star you are.*

And then, out of the corner of her eye, Nancy saw something move. She turned her head.

"Look at that!" cried Nancy. "It's a bear! A giant bear made out of stars!"

Nancy was so excited she got to her feet. "And look at that! Star fish swimming in a river of moonlight!" The bear leaned down and dipped his paw in the river. The fish scattered in a shower of stars.

Nancy turned her head again. "And there's an eagle!" yelled Nancy. "And a hunter with a bow

and arrow!" The hunter raised his bow. Nancy started jumping up and down. "Watch out!" she screamed.

The eagle rose. "Wow!" laughed Nancy. "This is better than telly."

CHAPTER FIVE

Nancy was playing hide and seek with the moon when her gran called her.

Nancy and the moon both looked down on Nancy's gran.
She was riding one
of Nancy's bikes.

"What is it?" asked Nancy.

"Your tea's ready," said her gran.

“Tea?” Nancy repeated. She’d forgotten about tea. “But I want to stay here. I’m having fun.”

"Then you've learned your lesson," said her gran. "It's time to come down."

"But I'll be bored again," said Nancy.

Nancy's gran held out her arms for Nancy to jump.

"Oh, you won't be bored, you've got plenty to do," said Nancy's gran.

"You have a houseful of toys to give away."